I0648834

Alfred Gurney

Parsifal

a festival play by Richard Wagner - a study

Alfred Gurney

Parsifal
a festival play by Richard Wagner - a study

ISBN/EAN: 9783337385712

Printed in Europe, USA, Canada, Australia, Japan

Cover: Foto ©Andreas Hilbeck / pixelio.de

More available books at **www.hansebooks.com**

PARSIFAL

A FESTIVAL PLAY BY RICHARD WAGNER

A STUDY

BY

ALFRED GURNEY, M.A.

VICAR OF S. BARNABAS', PIMLICO
AUTHOR OF 'OUR CATHOLIC INHERITANCE IN THE LARGER HOPE'
'THE VISION OF THE EUCHARIST' 'A CHRISTMAS FAGGOT' ETC.

'If any man among you seemeth to be wise in this world, let him become a fool, that he may be wise. For the wisdom of this world is foolishness with God'

'Blessed are the pure in heart, for they shall see God'

SECOND EDITION

LONDON
KEGAN PAUL, TRENCH, TRÜBNER, & CO. Ltd.
1892

(The rights of translation and of reproduction are reserved)

TO

HERBERT AND EDITH JEAFFRESON

IN HAPPY AND GRATEFUL MEMORY

OF AUGUST 1888

PARSIFAL

Glory and joy and honour to our Lord,
And to the Holy Vessel of the Grail.
                    TENNYSON, *The Holy Grail.*

ART is one of those oracles at whose shrine
the eager, anxious, inquisitive, aspiring intelligence of man is ever making enquiry. The
answers obtained are usually somewhat am-
biguous, never wholly satisfactory. Yet, at
certain golden periods of the world's history,
Art has spoken with a voice truly inspired.
It may be questioned whether the present century is one of those periods ; and the question is one that is likely, I think, to present
itself to all who have listened with attention

B

to Wagner's festival-play, ' Parsifal,' as performed at the only place where it can be heard—the Theatre of Bayreuth. It is the custom of his admirers to speak of the work of this illustrious composer as ' the music of the future '; and, indeed, if their estimate is right, the man whom they delight to honour is to be regarded, not so much as a composer, or even as a creator and inspirer, but rather as a discoverer and reformer, whose advent does not only mark a musical crisis, but inaugurates a new dispensation. There are others, no less worthy of attention, in whose judgment the popularity of Wagner is a passing fashion, and his influence not likely to leave a permanent or indelible mark behind it. I have no right even to an opinion, nor will I hazard so much as a conjecture, on a subject so warmly debated in the schools of music ; all I would venture to urge is this : let no one be over-confident in this controversy until he has heard 'Parsifal,' and given to Wagner's last, and confessedly greatest, achievement the careful examination that so remarkable a performance deserves.

While steering clear, however, of the musical controversy, and holding aloof alike from those who applaud him as a courageous reformer and those who condemn him as a reckless innovator, a lover of beauty may be permitted to render his tribute of homage to the man who has at least attempted, whether successfully or not, to marshal and combine all the arts in the interest of one supreme artistic endeavour, having for its object to present, with a measure of excellence approaching perfection, a drama altogether noble and ennobling. 'Our music,' says Emerson, 'our poetry, our language itself, are not satisfactions, but suggestions'; [1] but we cannot be too grateful to the artist whose aim

[1] *Essays*, 'Nature.'

is consistently lofty, and his work conscien-
tious. 'Art has not yet come to its maturity,'
to quote once again the Sage of Concord,
'if it do not put itself abreast with the
most potent influences of the world; if it is
not practical and moral; if it do not stand
in connection with the conscience; if it do
not make the poor and uncultivated feel
that it addresses them with a voice of lofty
cheer.'[1]

If we are to believe Mr. Haweis, the secret
of music's power is as yet undiscovered,
but he entertains the brightest hopes—hopes
which will be very generally shared by the
admirers of Wagner—as regards the destiny
of music in the near future. 'The day is at
hand,' he says, 'when the veil of the pro-
phetess will be lifted. Already in Germany,
the land of thought, music has been adopted
as the national art—as painting was once in

[1] *Essays*, ' Art.'

Italy, and sculpture in Greece. Already the names of Beethoven and Mozart are whispered through the civilized world in the same breath with those of Phidias and Michael Angelo, and the time is probably not far distant when music will stand revealed, perchance, as the mightiest of the arts, and certainly as the one art peculiarly representative of our modern world, with its intense life, complex civilization, and feverish self-consciousness.'[1] There are those, indeed, who say, and with much reason, that the endeavour to *express* anything by means of music is a futile and misdirected one; that music should be *impressive*, not *expressive*, and that in so far as it labours after expression it fails in impressiveness and dooms itself to impotence and failure. But without presuming either to endorse or to traverse this assertion, I shall surely carry with me all thoughtful worshippers in the temple of Art,

---

[1] *Music and Morals*, p. 10.

if I insist that it is not expression, but *repression*, that the 'feverish self-consciousness' of modern life demands at her hands. It is the high vocation of Art, and especially of music, not only to stimulate, but to *tranquillize*. It is so now no less than of old, when a shepherd-boy's simple instrument was found to be the minister of peace,—'When the evil spirit from God was upon Saul, then David took a harp and played with his hand: so Saul was refreshed and was well, and the evil spirit departed from him;'—and the modern orchestra, with all its manifold voices, is no less under obligation to exercise a salutary, soothing, and elevating influence. Such, assuredly, taken as a whole, is the aim and tendency of Wagner's 'Parsifal.'

If such conditions as those indicated by Emerson be applicable to the art of music, it may well be doubted whether any musical creation, ancient or modern, looked at in connection with the story that it accompanies, more adequately fulfils them. None will be found, I think, more triumphantly to justify the spiritual rapture of Browning's 'Abt Vogler,' expressed in the lines which, though familiar, I shall be pardoned for quoting :

All we have willed, or hoped, or dreamed of good, shall exist;
  Not its semblance, but itself; no beauty, nor good, nor power
Whose voice has gone forth, but each survives for the melodist
  When eternity confirms the conception of an hour.
The high that proved too high, the heroic for earth too hard,
  The passion that left the ground to lose itself in the sky,
Are music sent up to God by the lover and the bard ;
  Enough that He heard it once; we shall hear it by-and-bye.

And what is our failure here but a triumph's
    evidence
  For the fulness of the days ? Have we withered
    or agonized ?
Why else was the pause prolonged but that
    singing might issue thence ?
  Why rushed the discords in but that harmony
    should be prized ?
Sorrow is hard to bear, and doubt is slow to
    clear ;
  Each sufferer says his say, his scheme of the
    weal and woe :
But God has a few of us whom He whispers in
    the ear ;
  The rest may reason and welcome ; 'tis we
    musicians know.[1]

English readers, acquainted with Sir
Thomas Malory and Lord Tennyson, will at
first, perhaps, experience a feeling of disap-
pointment at hearing in 'Parsifal' nothing
of Arthur and his Queen, of Lancelot and
Galahad, of Merlin and Vivien, and the

[1] Dramatis Personæ, *Abt Vogler.*.

Knights of the Round Table; but we have only another part of the same endless story, enforcing the same lesson; and we are compensated for any regrets that we may not unnaturally feel, by a deepened sense of the ubiquity of the Divine Presence, meeting with the succours of Grace the manifold needs of man, and justifying and fulfilling all his highest aspirations; a Presence, however, that is clearly discerned, effectually appropriated, and vitally possessed, only by the dutiful, the single-hearted, and the pure. The Spanish Monsalvat, the scene of our play, no less than Camelot, Glastonbury, Tintagel, is a sanctuary of the Holy Grail. Every land visited by the Bride of Christ becomes a Palestine, a 'holy land'; wherever she has planted her feet and reared her altars the consecrating, beautifying Presence is vouchsafed; nay, it is enshrined in every humble, loving, and obedient heart. The earnest quest, the faithful custody of the Grail—is not this in truth always and everywhere the enterprise—the romance—of the Christian life? And nothing else than this is Art's truest inspiration. It is a joy to remember, as we follow the sublime story of 'Parsifal,' that in one of his last published letters Wagner makes an earnest and unhesitating profession of allegiance to Christ.

Wagner's festival-play is founded on a mediæval romance, the 'Parsifal' of Wolfram of Eschenbach, who died in 1230. It is observable that the customary five acts of a play are reduced to three; but the recognized features of the plot are carefully preserved. Act I. introduces the actors, makes us acquainted with a great enterprise, arrested by a serious reverse, and gives hope of ultimate success, as the vision of the Grail lays hands of benediction on the guileless heart of the entranced Parsifal, the predestined deliverer.

In Act II. the plot thickens, and the adversary, encouraged by the capture of the holy Spear, does his utmost to make good his success by the corruption of Parsifal and the plunder of the Grail; his magic and malice are, however, completely defeated by the valour and purity of the youthful champion. Act III. is the story of healing, recovery, and accomplished victory—the triumph of life and love over death and sin.

Again, the Dramatis Personæ are but six —five men and one woman. It may be well, as a preliminary to the interpretation of the story, if we attempt briefly to delineate these six characters. Each is a type and will repay careful study.

Titurel is the old king, who has abdicated in favour of his son Amfortas. To him, long years before, angels had committed 'the holy things,'—the sacred Cup of the Last Passover and the Spear that pierced the Saviour's

side. For their safe custody he had built a
sanctuary, the Castle of 'Monsalvat, and established the Brotherhood of the Grail's Keepers.
His heroic career at the time the play opens
has been long since concluded; it is no more
than a memory, but a memory that still stim-
ulates and inspires. The saintly old man lives
on, however, 'entombed in life by the grace of
God,' and sustained by the vision of the Grail
—a venerable presence, a voice of benediction.
The shadow of St. Joseph seems to rest upon
him, unforgetful of the angels' visit and the
sacred relics entrusted to his care. It is a
beautiful illustration of the ministry of old
age; of the hidden blessings that are silently
multiplied under its benignant shadow. Be-
reft of the heavenly vision through the sin of
his son, the reigning King Amfortas, he dies
before the third Act opens, and his funeral
procession adds a significant solemnity to the
closing scene, when the Grail, again unveiled

in the hands of Parsifal, has power to lift him for a moment from his coffin—an indication of the resurrection life upon which he has already entered.

To Gurnemanz belongs another kind of ministry. He is a Knight of the Grail, old, but still vigorous; a man of great courage, devotion, and integrity; not, however, gifted with any large measure of spiritual insight, as is shown by his misinterpreting Parsifal's silent ecstasy when the Grail is revealed at the end of the first Act, and his disallowing Kundry's gracious offer of service at the beginning of the third. He represents the large class of well-meaning people to whom the idealist is ever a puzzle, often an offence; who fail to understand that spiritual wisdom is the child rather of intuition and reflection than of observation; who, though in the kingdom of the Spirit, walk rather by sight than faith, and are slow to discern the things which can be seen only by the aid of that sevenfold light that illuminates the holy place. It is the mission of Gurnemanz, like the man with the pitcher of water in the Gospel, to conduct others to the banquet hall; to introduce, like St. John the Baptist, one greater than himself. By his loyalty and uprightness he helps to keep alive the high tradition of the Brotherhood, and his hermit life is an eloquent protest against the laxity which threatens to involve the holy enterprise to which they are pledged in irreparable disaster. Parsifal receives baptism, anointing, and investiture as a Knight of the Grail at his hands.

Amfortas is King of the Brotherhood and guardian of the Grail. He is disabled by an ever-bleeding wound, and his pallid and beautiful countenance wears habitually an expression of sorrowful dejection, intensified at last into the anguish of despair. For he has failed to fulfil his high mission, and is paralysed by the consciousness of sin unabsolved. He has, in fact, yielded to the fascinations of Kundry, 'a maid of fearful beauty,' and, enslaved by her, has failed to retain possession of the holy Spear, the true defence of the Grail. This is the weapon which, wielded by the hand of the magician Klingsor, has punished his infidelity and inflicted the wound that makes him long for death. Conscience-stricken and unshriven he fears to handle the Grail, any approach to which aggravates his aching wound; and when at length he is encouraged to unveil the holy Cup by the command of Titurel, and the oracular words that promise the advent of a deliverer, he still shrinks from participating in the sacred Feast. He is plunged in a very abyss of sorrow, like Peter when he went forth from the Presence-chamber and wept bitterly. It is the sadness that takes possession of a man's heart when, conscience being still alive and awake, he knows himself accountable for a mission frustrated, a vocation forfeited.

Klingsor, on the other hand, is a hardened miscreant—a sinner whose conscience is seared; a deliberate corrupter of others, in league with the powers of darkness. Kundry is bound to him by a curse against which she rebels, but from which she is powerless to extricate herself; the flower-maidens are his willing tools; the recreant knights his deluded victims. He had sought once to be enrolled in the Brotherhood of the Grail, and had been rejected, being found unworthy; hence his persistent hostility—a man of reprobate mind, hateful and hating. He overreaches himself, however, as is the fashion of his kind, and, plotting the capture of the Grail, loses the Spear. Aimed at the heart of Parsifal, it falls to his hand, and when he makes with

it the sign of the Cross, the whole kingdom of Klingsor, in which nothing is real, nothing substantial, falls to pieces and utterly
perishes. Like Judas he goes to his own
place.

There is, perhaps, more of delicacy and
subtlety in the delineation of Kundry than of
any other character in the play. She is the
child of Nature, the creature of impulse, a
woman always instinctively seeking satisfac-
tion in service and self-sacrifice, and not
without high aspirations even when most
wayward and reckless. We are permitted to
watch the development of this wild, undisciplined being—at first little more than an
animal—until, delivered from the curse that
bound and tortured her by Parsifal's deter-
mined resistance to the evil spirit that
possessed her, she learns to possess her soul
in patience, and in lowliest, loveliest penitence
offers at the feet of the Absolver and Restorer

the fragrant oblation of a dedicated heart. It is a beautiful transfiguration; all the passionate, untamed impulses of the pagan woman are brought under the yoke of loving obedience, and harnessed like horses of fire to the Gospel chariot. She is baptized by Parsifal, and is thenceforth, no less than himself, a devoted servant of the Holy Grail.

It is on the very steps of the altar that she falls, when, at the end, Parsifal uplifts the sacred Chalice; and the dim whiteness of the upturned face, as her eyes close in death, looks like a lovely reflection of the descending Dove, heaven's holy bird, that hovers above his head. She is one of those who follow in the steps of Mary Magdalene—all daughters of Jerusalem, all servants of the Grail. Let no one fail to observe that it is Kundry, and Kundry only, who knows the story of Parsifal's birth and childhood. It is she who tells him of his mother, Heart's Affliction, a true mother of sorrows, whose heart was broken by the desolations of widowhood and the loss of her only child; it is she who first suspects the meaning of the mystic name *Parsifal*—a name which his father Gamuret, when dying on the field of battle, had given to his unborn babe, and which had escaped from his mother's lips while buried in a prophetic dream. Truly does Gurnemanz say of Kundry that she 'knows many things': she knows the bitterness of sin, the dissatisfaction of self-pleasing, the joy of conversion, the sweetness of penitence, the dignity of service, the beatitude of sacrifice, the inspiration of love.

Parsifal is the hero of our story; he is not only the son of Heart's Affliction, but also Wisdom's child,—humble, guileless, loving, pure, and *a fool*. Not only do the wanton flower-maidens deride his folly, but Gurnemanz also, and Kundry; nay, he is ready enough to acknowledge the truth of the impeachment; he calls himself 'a timid fool.' To bring so hasty an accusation is, in such cases, the way of the world; for Parsifal is an idealist—a man of intuition. But that is not all: 'his strength is as the strength of ten, because his heart is pure,'—pure with the inviolate Christian purity, not of ice, but of fire. He is ignorant enough at first, and his path lies through failure and error, as well as through strife and sorrow; but he is quick to learn the lesson of every reverse, and to do penance for every offence: and so his life is an ascent and a victory, until at last he is perfectly initiated into the spiritual science— the true philosophy of life of which love holds the key—and fulfilled of that divine folly, self-abnegation, upon which the world pours scorn but which in the kingdom of realities goes by the name of *wisdom*. Parsifal is an elect vessel—the child of a God-given destiny —

and he accomplishes his mission; to the sin-
stricken and despairing Amfortas, to Kundry
the world-weary and desolate, he brings the
succours of compassion. A true paraclete, a
good Samaritan, furnished with oil and wine
to soothe and stimulate, he becomes, by
his gift of sympathy, the bearer of the
burdens of others and the healer of their
wounds. Such is Parsifal at the end of the
play—the selfless man, the perfect Knight, the
King of Monsalvat, the guardian of the Grail,
the servant and image of Christ. But at the
beginning, he is, no less than Kundry herself,
the creature of undisciplined impulse, recognizing no law because wholly guileless, and
ignorant of sin which it connotes and ineffec-
tually condemns. His gradual development
—a true pilgrim's progress—is indicated with
much imaginative subtlety. Remorse at the
death of the slaughtered swan—a ' trespass '
committed in ignorance of the sacredness of

life; recognition of a conflict in the world between good and evil, when Kundry tells him
that the giants and caitiffs he had slain were
wicked; desolation of heart when informed
of the death of his forsaken mother; the
vision of the Grail, which he beholds in awe-
struck silence, and which seems never after-
wards to fade from his eyes; and the awakening of compassion when the agonized cry of
Amfortas falls on his ear;—these are the
crises of a growing illumination in the first
stage of his spiritual development. Then, in
the second Act, comes a threefold conflict,
in which, though sore-beset, he comes off victorious. It is the mystery of temptation—a
necessary experience in the educational process
—with which all must become acquainted who
are predestined to perfection. His gallantry
achieves an easy victory over the apostate
Knights of the Grail, the dupes of Klingsor, and
his flower-maidens. Nor do the seductions of

these fascinating but frivolous damsels seri-
ously imperil his honour and virtue; but,
when the same temptation presents itself
in a subtier and more spiritual form, recom-
mended by Kundry's plausible arguments,
passionate appeals, and intoxicating beauty,
for a moment the issue seems to tremble in
the balance. He is saved by the spear-wound
of sudden compunction which (mindful of
Amfortas) he feels burning, bleeding in his
heart, and by the never-forgotten vision of
the holy Cup, bringing with it the memory
of the Redeemer's Passion. He falls on his
knees and prays, and thus fortified, when
Kundry renews her endearments, spurns her
from him. The snare is broken, and he is
delivered. At the end, all is peace and purity;
it is the time of love, the day of redemption.
Parsifal has wandered far, and suffered much;
he has grown at length into spiritual manhood. We see him purified by prayer and

consecrated by chrism ; baptized, anointed, invested in white tunic and red mantle as King of Monsalvat. Thus richly endowed and fully equipped he exercises a redemptive ministry, baptizes Kundry, heals with the recovered Spear the wound of Amfortas, and, before the eyes of the assembled Brotherhood, uplifts the Sacrament of Benediction.

Such are the actors in this sacred drama. In the endeavour to delineate Parsifal, and to indicate the progressive stages of his spiritual growth, I have already anticipated no small portion of the story; it may be well now, however, to return to the commencement, and give in briefest outline a sketch of the entire play.

ACT I.

O music-marvel ! how your royal river
Mirrors our life ; there breathes exhaled from it
Sorrow and joy, and triumph and despair.
RODEN NOEL, *Beethoven.*

THE overture, which occupies a quarter of
an hour, is unspeakably solemn, plaintive,
urgent, impressive ; at times heart-piercing as
a woman's wail, and then again reassuring
as the trumpet-peals of a conquering army,
jubilant as the *Te Deum* that celebrates a
victory. The Grail *motif* is simplicity itself,
and once heard can never be forgotten.[1]
Then the curtain opens on a very lovely

---

[1] The Grail *motif* is not entirely new ; the second half
is called the 'Dresden Amen,' as it is used at the Dresden
Hof Kirche. It is also used by Mendelssohn in his Re-
formation Symphony.

scene—a forest, with a low-lying lake in the distance. It recalls the first lines of Dante's 'Inferno.' But, though sombre, the forest is not sad; sunbeams penetrate its shade, and birds build their nests in its shelter and make music in its branches. Life makes us acquainted with many tragedies, but a tragedy itself it is not; if it seem so to us, it is because we see only a fragment. The sunshine that penetrates even to its darkest, deepest abysses bears witness to a never-forsaking Love whereby it is evermore encompassed, cherished, quickened; the waters of purification are within sight, and the joy-song of creation, breathing hope, is never wholly silenced.

Under a tree three sleepers are seen—Gurnemanz and two esquires. Roused by a solemn morning reveille of trombones from the castle, they fall on their knees, and, as the sun rises, engage in silent prayer. The

drama begins and ends with prayer and
in silence.

Two Knights enter, and they fall to speak-
ing of Amfortas, his shattered health and
unclosed wound. Sorrowfully Gurnemanz
declares that there is but one remedy—'One
thing is needful—one Man'—apart from which,
hope there is none. Reliance is placed on
two remedies, which promise at least allevia-
tion, but to no purpose: (1) A bath in the
consecrated lake, the haunt of swans; (2)
a balsam brought by Kundry in a crystal
flask from Arabia. But water unmingled
with blood is of no avail for a sin-wounded
heart; and it is God's cup alone that holds
the healing balsam.

Kundry's entrance is startling; in loose
garb and snake-skin girdle, with wild eyes
and black, flowing locks, she rushes in, her
mare having fallen on the threshold—a
frenzied woman. She hands the flask to

Gurnemanz, and flings herself down on the ground. Thus is Nature personified—Nature, disordered and defiant, not yet redeemed and reconciled, whose impulses are passionate rather than impassioned, whose methods are forcible rather than effectual. Yet has Gurnemanz discernment enough to recognize in her impetuosity some measure of faith and zeal, and a sincere, though fitful, desire to serve the disheartened Brotherhood and the disconsolate King.

Amfortas is borne in on a litter ; he thanks Kundry for the balsam, and proceeds down the valley for his bath in the lake. While he is so occupied Gurnemanz relates to the youths who attend him the story of Klingsor and his infamous magic ; how, by a woman's 'fearful beauty' (for, if he knows the part she had played, he is careful to screen Kundry), he had bewitched the King, and won from him the sacred Spear. He concludes by

recounting the broken and oracular words
that had given promise of recovery and
deliverance :

>   There, at the plundered sanctuary,
>   In prayer impassioned knelt Amfortas,
>   Imploring for a sign of safety :
> A heavenly radiance from the Grail then floated ;
>   A sacred phantom face
>   From lips divine did chase
> These words, whose purpose clearly could be
>   noted :—
>   By pity 'lightened
>   A guileless fool ;
>   Wait for him, my chosen tool.[1]

The words are repeated with deep awe by
the listeners, when suddenly they are inter-

---

[1] *Parsifal*, p. 14. English translation by H. L. and F.
Corder. ‘By sympathy made wise ’ would be a more accurate
rendering of the eighth line ; but it is difficult in a translation to give the full force and meaning of the original.
This is the German :

> ‘ Durch Mitleid wissend,
>   der reine Thor ;
>   harre sein,
>   den ich erkor.’

rupted by cries of horror, as a wild swan flutters from over the lake and falls dead before them. Parsifal, armed with bow and arrows—a very David for comeliness and strength—is immediately discovered and con-victed of having aimed the death-blow. The scene that follows is very striking. Parsifal makes no defence; 'eagle-like' himself, he has been in the habit of defending his life against the assaults of fierce eagles and wolves, meaning no wrong. 'I hit all that flies'—that is his rule; he has had as yet no vision of the Lamb and the Dove or he would surely have spared the swan. He is quick to learn the lesson of mercy, and, conscience-stricken, breaks his bow and flings away his arrows.

The episode of the swan may seem to some ludicrous, not I think to anyone possessed of artistic insight. It has its bearing, no doubt, on the morality of sport; not, I submit, in the

sense of unqualified censure and condemna-
tion, but indicating that dwellers on God's
Holy Mountain (for the deed was done in the
Grail's domain) hurt not nor destroy, but
reverence and cherish animal life ; beasts there
are 'safe and sacred,' 'friendly and fond ' ;
the child may with impunity play on the hole
of the asp, for in that high country men and
animals have ceased to devour, have learnt to
serve, one another. But the incident carries
with it a lesson of wider application, and
administers a rebuke to that evil spirit (not
to be called scientific, for it is the degrada-
tion and prostitution of science) which must
be held responsible for the countless atrocities
perpetrated in the Continental schools of vivi-
section. It is a consolation to add a name so
illustrious as that of Wagner to those of Rus-
kin, Tennyson, Browning, and many others,
representative of the highest artistic intelligence of the century, and conspicuous on the

roll of those who have raised an earnest and indignant protest against a system as profane, and apparently as profitless, as it is cruel.　In the earthly paradise it is ever man's duty (as it was Adam's) to call the animals by name, and, accepting their service, to serve them in return, ruling, protecting, educating, them; impious is the hand that inflicts upon them needless torture, debauched the heart that is indifferent to their dumb anguish.

God made all the creatures, and gave them our
　　love and our fear,
To give sign, we and they are His children, one
　　family here.[1]

To return to our play.　Parsifal, questioned as to his home, his father, his business, declares his ignorance. 'Thy name, then?' enquires Gurnemanz. 'I once had many, but now I know not one of them,' he replies.

　　　　[1] Browning, *Saul*.

Kundry, also, it should be observed, has had many names, and Klingsor reminds her of them at the beginning of the next Act. Until the work of unification is wrought in a man's self, he plays many parts, not one of them successfully. Parsifal was awaiting the bestowal of the 'new name'—that name the meaning of which no man knows until he corresponds to it, his purified heart the 'white stone' prepared for its inscription. It is not till the middle of the second Act, in the midst of fiery trial, that it is made known to him. One thing, however, Parsifal knows:

I have a mother, Heart's Affliction she's hight;

and when Kundry informs him of her premature death, he turns upon her in anger, and being restrained by Gurnemanz, faints away. Water from the brook, quickly brought by the ever-ready hands of Kundry, restores him. Each incident marks a step in the rapid growth of

D

his spiritual intelligence ; with lips moistened
by a woman's gracious ministry, and a heart
enlarged by the discipline of sorrow, he puts
to Gurnemanz the tremendous question—
' What is the Grail ? ' For him the time of
awakening has arrived ; the quest has begun ;
nor is he daunted by the reply :

> No earthly road to it doth lead ;
> By no one can it be detected
> Who by Itself is not elected.[1]

Space and time are now felt to be an
illusion ; for the veil is being lifted before his
eyes, his feet are treading with glad alacrity
the ascending path of aspiration, and the day-
star of spiritual desire has arisen in his heart.
The scene changes—the music resembles a
rushing, mighty wind, a heavenly tempest
which seems to shake and blend the palpitat-
ing earth and the stooping heavens, and to

[1] Corder, p. 21.

build and fashion the temple that gradually
emerges from the darkness. The forest dis-
appears; long-sustained trombone notes softly
swell; approaching peals of bells are heard.
At last they arrive at a mighty hall, which
loses itself overhead in a high, vaulted dome,
from which alone the light streams in. I
despair of doing justice to the beauty of the
scene that follows. The Knights of the Grail
enter in solemn procession, and take their
places at a table placed circle-wise and furnished with silver cups, an altar standing in
the midst. They proceed to chant the hymn
of the Holy Supper, answered first by the
voices of the youths from the mid-height of
the hall, and again by a second invisible choir
of boys from the summit of the dome:

His love endures,
The Dove upsoars,
The Saviour's sacred token;

D 2

Take the wine red,
For you 'twas shed,
Let Bread of Life be broken.[1]

Then enters Amfortas, borne on a litter, and preceded by the procession of the Holy Grail; the shrine draped in purple is placed on the altar. A long silence follows, broken at length by the voice of Titurel, who speaks unseen from behind the throne of Amfortas 'as from a grave,' and bids him uncover the Grail. This, after long hesitation, he is persuaded to do, emboldened by the oracular words already quoted, which float down from the dome, sung by the heavenly choir. No sooner is the Grail, an antique crystal cup, revealed, than a ray of light shoots down from above, causing it to glow with a ruddy lustre, 'a rose-red sparkle.' As Amfortas uplifts it, all fall upon their knees. Then it

[1] Corder, p. 23.

is again veiled and returned to the shrine.
A sacramental meal follows, the serving boys
receiving a benediction from the altar upon
the gifts they dispense, pass down the tables,
filling the silver cups with wine and distribut-
ing to each of the Knights a piece of bread.
It is an action full of solemn and impressive
beauty; the servants of the Grail, in their
graceful and measured movements, recalling
the angels of Botticelli. The choristers of
the dome commence the sacramental hymn,
which is taken up again by the youths from the
middle height, and continued by the Knights.

Blessed believing; Blessed in loving

are the concluding words sung by the whole
choir. Then the processions are re-formed;
Amfortas is borne out pressing his hand to his
aching wound, preceded by the Grail; and the
Knights, saluting one another with the kiss of
peace, retire.

And then the music faded, and the Grail
Passed, and the beam decayed, and from the walls
The rosy quiverings died into the night.[1]

Gurnemanz and Parsifal alone remain. The latter has stood spellbound and motionless throughout the whole scene. Gurnemanz addresses him in ill-humour: 'Why standest thou there? Wist thou what thou sawest?' Parsifal shakes his head, and Gurnemanz rejoins, 'Thou art, then, nothing but a fool! In future leave our swans in peace, and seek, gander, your goose.' It is an old German proverb signifying 'go and find the wife fit for you'; here the meaning is 'go and live the life of the world;—the consecrated life, the counsels of perfection, the guardianship of the Grail, are not for you.' With these contemptuous words Gurnemanz opens a side door, and, not without some show of violence, dis-

---

[1] Tennyson, *The Holy Grail.*

misses Parsifal. Immediately the voice of a
chorister is heard from above singing again the
oracular words of promise, and Gurnemanz
pauses for a moment and looks up ; but he
is in no humour to ' wait ' and ponder their
meaning, and so the timely warning is lost
upon him ; he goes out, little dreaming that
he has turned his back upon the predestined
restorer, the chosen vessel of God's grace and
the instrument of His saving purpose. Once
again, as the curtain closes, the choir sing,
to the music of the Grail *motif*, the words
' Blessed in faith, blessed in love '—a twofold
benediction which, we may be sure, brings
consolation to the heart of the insulted and
bewildered Parsifal. It is something like the
salutation wherewith Mary, on the threshold
of that cloistered home in the valley of the
terebinths, heard herself greeted by her cousin
Elizabeth.

ACT II.

Here the blot is blanched
By God's gift of a purity of soul
That will not take pollution, ermine-like,
Armed from dishonour by its own soft snow.
Such was the gift of God who showed for once
How He would have the world go white.

Why comes temptation but for man to meet
And master and make crouch beneath his foot,
And so be pedestalled in triumph ?
BROWNING, *The Ring and the Book.*

THE first Act is much the longest of the
three ; it closes in awe-struck silence—there
is no applause—and is followed by an hour's
interval. All too soon the silver trumpets
summon the audience to resume their places,
and, as the curtains part, we are introduced
to the magic castle of Klingsor, full of ne-
cromantic appliances, with heavy chains for

chamber ornaments and with steps descending
into a dark pit. Klingsor himself is gazing
into a metal mirror; for the lost world to
which he belongs is an unsubstantial one—
a phantom world—upon which only shadows
fall—the evidence of realities out of sight, on
the other side of which the sun is shining.
He burns incense, and a white vapour arises
from the pit, revealing at length the veiled
form of Kundry, obedient to the summons.
An altercation ensues, Klingsor holding her
bound by the spell, from which only he who
resists her ensnaring fascinations can release
her, and she, now mocking, now wailing, in
a desperate attempt to extricate herself from
his power. 'Weak all men,' she exclaims,
' by my curse and with me all of them perish
. . . oh, woe is me!' They are disturbed
by a clash of arms heard from without, and
Klingsor, mounting the rampart, has the
mortification of seeing the recreant knights,

who garrison his castle, routed by Parsifal. With a cry of anguish Kundry vanishes in the mouth of the pit, and for a few seconds there is complete darkness. When the light returns it reveals, in place of the vanished castle, a flower-garden, rich in the colour of tropical vegetation. Parsifal is seen approaching, flushed with victory, smiling and radiant, and finds himself at once surrounded by a bevy of flower-maidens, outraged for the moment by the loss of their lovers, the defeated knights, but quickly appeased by his undisguised and wondering admiration. They dance round him, advancing and retreating with enticing words and gestures, and the lovely music that accompanies seems to inspire and justify their gambols. Parsifal, dazzled and delighted, is at first disposed to join in what he deems their child-like and innocent play; but soon he detects their wantonness, and, just as he is about to free himself from their importunities by flight, he is suddenly arrested, and they are affrighted and scattered, by the voice of Kundry heard from a flowery recess, calling him—the name-less one—by name. So these foolish and frivolous damsels, in whose laughter is no gladness, fade away and disappear. ' Flower-maidens' they call themselves, but they are neither flowers nor women; had they been either they had been beautiful; but beauty may not be had divorced from truth and virtue, nor realized in masquerade. They bloom in a magical garden, they belong to a phantom-world, as unsubstantial as sin itself. We are permitted, however, to believe that they, too, in the sequel—in the ultimate issue —emerge into the world of realities, quickened, like Kundry herself, by Parsifal's repulse; for, in the final Act, he draws attention to the flowering meadows fertilized by their peniten-tial tears.

Our hero finds himself now in the presence
of a more formidable danger. The scene that
follows is marked by much discriminating delicacy; the thought is suggested—and it is a
serious consideration for us all—that we are
most likely to tempt, and to be tempted by,
those with whom we have most in common,
who are able to touch us at the springs of
thought and feeling, in the very depths and
recesses of our being; all the more if the
common interest be intrinsically worthy and
legitimately attractive. The impulsive gene-
rosity of Kundry's passionate nature renders
her solicitation a snare exceptionally perilous
to a heart so unsuspicious, so accessible to
affection, as Parsifal's—a heart that no selfish
or worthless woman would have any power
to corrupt. For Kundry, even when con-
strained by the curse that is upon her to play
the part of a temptress, is still an aspirant; she
would persuade herself, as well as Parsifal, that

their passion is lawful, as was that of his
parents when first their young hearts yielded
to the witchery of love; and when this subtle
suggestion fails, she desperately insists that
by the indulgence of their love salvation may
be wrought. It is the common delusion—the
familiar error of the carnal man, who deems
that the goal of life may be reached by
crooked paths and in the pursuit of selfish
aims. But self-sacrifice, not self-gratification,
is the Divine principle, the saving principle,
the *life* principle, and by his steadfast, unswerv-
ing allegiance to it, Parsifal saves, not himself
only, but the woman who tempts him. The
Spear and the Chalice, representing mortification and spiritual quickening, are the potent
memories that ever abide with him, and the
thought of them, and of Him whose they
are, supervenes to protect him in the hour
of fiery trial. It is the familiar drama of
temptation in one of its most familiar forms;

but seldom has the great lesson of self-conquest for the love of Christ been more eloquently and persuasively enforced.

In our examination of the spiritual education of Parsifal and Kundry I have been led to remark upon several points of resemblance, but there is something of contrast too, typical of an often-recognized difference between man and woman, which an attentive observer will not fail to mark. It is Kundry who, in the moment of defeat and deepest humiliation, discovers the hunger of her soul, and speaks of the Divine Lover whom she dare not invoke: 'I saw Him: mocked Him! I caught then His glance; I seek Him now from world to world.'[1] It is the passionate wail of the

---

[1] It may be that an idea like that which we associate with the story of the Wandering Jew is in the poet's mind. May I remind my readers of a fine poem by Buchanan, the *Ballad of Judas Iscariot*, in which he describes the restless wanderings of the conscience-stricken traitor, and the blessed goal at which they terminate

forlorn woman's yearning heart. Women are
the first to go on the holy quest; they are
seekers before men; they head the procession
to Cross and Sepulchre; and with them the
incentive—the constraining, stimulating force
—is more often personal devotion. Men are
more under the sway of ideas—more rational,
more deliberate, less emotional, less intuitive;
they are apt to seek a deliverance rather
than a deliverer. Something of this may, I
think, be detected, if we compare Parsifal
with Kundry.

There is yet another point well worthy of
attention. Parsifal's temptation, so victori-
ously resisted, quickens and intensifies within
him the desire to serve and help the defeated
and suffering King—' Shew me the way to
Amfortas,' is his appeal both to Kundry and
Gurnemanz. A divine pity has penetrated
and taken possession of his heart. That he
should stand in need of a guide is also

observable.   The man who brings redemption
is usually one who needs another to prepare his
way before him, and it is the honourable and
privileged ministry of the man of observation
and practical sagacity, acquainted with ways
and means, albeit deficient in the penetration
that belongs to a keen spiritual intelligence, to
be the herald and forerunner of the deliverer,
the success of whose enterprise depends largely
on the fidelity with which this work of prepara-
tion has been performed.

With Kundry's discomfiture the second
Act quickly closes.   Desperate at the failure
of his accomplice, Klingsor appears poising
a lance, and challenges Parsifal:

Halt! there.   I'll ban thee with befitting gear,
The Fool shall perish by his Master's spear.[1]

Thus is the axe laid to the root of the tree.
He aims the Spear at Parsifal; it swerves,

---

[1] Corder, p. 48.

angel-guided, and Parsifal, grasping it with a look of rapture, makes with it the sign of the Cross. The effect is instantaneous: as with the shock of an earthquake the castle falls into ruins and the flower-garden withers up to a desert. Kundry falls with a shriek, and Parsifal, as he departs, regarding her with a look of compassion, speaks the last word—' Thou know'st where only we shall meet again.' There is, in truth, only one place of rendezvous for the weary, wistful, shivering hearts of bewildered men—at the feet—in the arms—of the Son of Man, the Child of Obedience, the King of Love, the Lord of Life. 'The world passeth away and the lust thereof, but he that doeth the Will of God abideth for ever.'

ACT III.

Around the vase of Life at your slow pace
   He has not crept, but turned it with his hands,
   And a'l its sides already understands.
There, girt, one breathes alert for some great race ;
Whose road runs far by sands and fruitful space ;
   Who laughs, yet through the jolly throng has pass'd ;
   Who weeps, nor stays for weeping ; who at last,
A youth, stands somewhere crowned, with silent face.
            D. G. ROSSETTI, *The Vase of Life.*

ANOTHER long interval intervenes between the
second and third Acts, and we find, on resum-
ing our seats, that in the progress of the play
a considerable period has elapsed. Gurnemanz appears as a venerable hermit, though
still wearing the tunic of a Knight of the
Grail; and Parsifal has grown from a mere
stripling to ripe manhood. But the greatest
change is in Kundry. The thorny thicket

which has been for so long her lair—her grave [1]
—is now forsaken; for her the winter has at
length passed, the spring has arrived. She,
who formerly longed only for death, longs now
only-for service—the service of a dedicated
life, given to God in lowliest worship, to man

[1] Very pathetic in the early part of the play is the
craving of the restless soul for rest. The slumber that
visits her is no healthy, natural, recreative sleep; it brings
with it a foretaste of the helplessness, the bitterness, the
terror of death. It is a kind of grave into which she sinks
shuddering—a grave where the evil spell under whose
dominion she has fallen immediately becomes operative;
and when she wakes it is in the world of unrealities.
Some have thought that Adam's sleep (Genesis ii. 21)
was of this character—one of the ' sundry kinds of death,'
a spiritual lethargy resulting from the indulgence of a
misdirected desire for fellowship other than that which
he had with God. It was, they imagine, a first fall and
failure when he sought among the creatures for a help-
meet for him. The deep sleep ' immediately followed
and the separation of sex; the result being that man lived
a divided life until in Christ, the New Man, the Second
Adam, human nature was repaired and reinstated, and the
breach effectually healed. See Gal. iii. 28. S. John xix.
34. The patristic interpretations of this passage are given
in a valuable ' additional note ' of Westcott's *Commentary*
on S. John, p. 284.

in tenderest ministry. It is in truth a *new* Kundry that we see, more than transfigured, re-created after a Divine pattern, and conformed to a Divine image. If we are right in regarding her as a representation of Nature, the story suggests more than one valuable lesson. Never without good impulses, she is at first powerless to pursue any consistent course, restless and hungry-hearted, now mocking, now mourning; at one time deriding the 'witless fool,' at another doing homage to his uprightness and valour. Sadly the words fall from her lips, 'I never rest; I do no good thing. Alas! I am weary.'

> With eyes aglow, and aimless zeal,
>   She hither, thither, goes;
> Her speech, her motions, all reveal
>   A mind without repose.
>
> The demons blast her to and fro;
>   She has no quiet place;
> Enough a woman still to know
>   A haunting, dim disgrace.

Hers in no other eyes confide
    For even a moment brief ;
With restless glance they turn aside,
    Lest they betray her grief.[1]

Such is the condition to which disobedience has reduced human nature. But where sin has abounded, Grace has much more abounded. The days of Kundry's bondage and dishonour are at length numbered and ended ; her feet, after long and weary wanderings, are now at last duteously climbing the slopes of the Mountain of Purification, its ' pure air, of the sweet colour of the oriental sapphire,' fanning her brow, and its glad songs finding an echo in her engraced and emancipated heart. She is at last clothed and in her right mind ; a child of the Kingdom whose laws are beatitudes. Only one word she utters in the third Act— the murmured aspiration of a woman's heart

[1] George MacDonald, *Poems.*

established in the humility of abiding contrition : 'Service ! Service !' We may, perhaps, transfer to her silent lips the words (written during music) of a modern poet :

Oh ! what is this that knows the road I came,
The flame turned cloud, the cloud returned to flame,
  The lifted shifted steeps and all the way ?—
That draws round me at last this wind-warm space,
And in regenerate rapture turns my face
  Upon the devious coverts of dismay ? [1]

Kundry, piloted by cloud and flame, like the pilgrim Church of old, has found at length her holy land of promise, where the Spirit's breath is warm, and the smile of God manifest.

And in Parsifal, no less than in Kundry, we may discern the evolution of the New Man,—the gradual upgrowth and development of that which springs from an incorrup-

---

[1] D. G. Rossetti, *The Monochord.*

tible seed, and attains at length, fostered by
salutary resistance, to the full measure of the
stature of Christ. Both come out of much
tribulation : both, though in ways so differ-
ent, become acquainted with the mystery of
iniquity, both are goaded by 'the conscience-
prick and the memory-sting'; both at last,
cross-laden, wounded, and victorious, are
brought forth into a wealthy place; made
citizens of that spiritual City whose walls are
named Salvation, and her gates Praise.

When, for the third time, the curtain is
drawn, we find ourselves back in the Grail's
domain ; it is daybreak, as at the beginning ;
but instead of the forest-lake in the back-
ground there are flowery meadows bathed
in dew ; in the foreground a spring of pellucid
water ;—it is a scene of peaceful beauty, as
befits 'the ever-hallowed Good Friday morn,'
for once again the day of victory has dawned.
Parsifal enters, a black knight in complete

armour. Pacing slowly, with measured step
and dignified bearing, he seems to realize
Wordsworth's conception of 'The Happy
Warrior'—calm and strong with the happiness that does not exclude but ennobles
sorrow :

> Who, doomed to go in company with pain,
> And fear, and bloodshed, miserable train !
> Turns his necessity to glorious gain ;
> In face of these doth exercise a power
> Which is our human nature's highest dower ;
> Controls them and subdues, transmutes, bereaves
> Of their bad influence, and their good receives ;
> By objects, which might force the soul to abate
> Her feeling, rendered more compassionate ;
> Is placable, because occasions rise
> So often that demand such sacrifice ;
> More skilful in self-knowledge, even more pure,
> As tempted more ; more able to endure,
> As more exposed to suffering and distress ;
> Thence also more alive to tenderness.
>
> Whom neither shape of danger can dismay,
> Nor thought of tender happiness betray ;

Who, not content that former worth stand fast,
Looks forward, persevering to the last,
From well to better, daily self-surpassed.

Gurnemanz does not at first recognize him,
and, still a reprover, remonstrates with him
for bearing arms on so holy a day. Parsifal
in silence plants his spear in the ground, lays
down his sword and shield, removes his
helmet, and kneels down in prayer. On ris-
ing he gives his hand to Gurnemanz, and tells
the story of his many wanderings, sufferings,
and conflicts—the guardian of the Grail's most
holy Spear :

> In its behalf, in its safe warding,
> I won from every weapon a wound.[1]

Gurnemanz tells him how, since their last
meeting, trouble has increased,—Amfortas,
afraid to fulfil his sacred office, the vision of the
Grail lost, the holy meal denied them, Titurel
dead, and the Brotherhood utterly dispirited,

[1] Corder, p. 53.

their hopes frustrated, their strength withered, their cause lost. Parsifal is overcome with grief, and at the point of fainting; Gurnemanz supports and leads him to a seat on the grassy knoll beside the spring. One beautiful incident follows another; every gesture is graceful, every word gracious. Kundry, removing his greaves, with cherishing hands bathes his feet; Gurnemanz baptizes him with water from the spring; Kundry anoints his feet with ointment from the golden flask, and, stooping low, wipes them with her lovely hair. Gurnemanz anoints his head, and declares him King; and, finally, Parsifal baptizes Kundry, and, tenderly regarding her, deliberately and reverently kisses her on the forehead. In sympathy with man, all creatures seem to rejoice, 'through God's love-sacrifice made clean and pure'; and Nature, on this holy day of redemption and restitution, with sun-smile and bird-song and flower-fragrance, uplifts her voice and offers her oblation of glad thanksgiving.

> The world's unwithered countenance
> Is bright as on Creation's day.[1]

Parsifal, in an exalted mood of trustful assurance and tranquil rapture, discerns in Kundry the first-fruits of a world-harvest, and confidently anticipates the salvation even of the fickle and heartless flower-maidens :

> I saw my scornful mockers wither ;
> Now look they for forgiveness hither ;
> Like a sweet dew a tear from thee, too, floweth :
> Thou weepest—see ! the landscape gloweth.[2]

Baptized and anointed, Parsifal is now ready for investiture as Knight and King of

---

[1] Goethe, *Faust.*

[2] Corder, p. 58. The following is a literal (and I think preferable) translation :

> ' I saw them fade who laughed once to me ;
> (I wonder) whether to-day they long for salvation ;
> Thy tears also have turned to dew of blessing,
> Thou weepest—see, the meadows laugh.'

the Grail. The hands of Gurnemanz and Kundry blessedly meet as they clothe him with the sacred mantle embroidered with the soaring Dove, the symbol of spiritual power.

And now the scene changes as in the first Act, and we find ourselves once more in the sanctuary of the Grail. The bells are sweetly and solemnly pealing. Two processions enter; one is a funeral procession, the Knights escorting the coffin of Titurel, ' sovereign father,' saint and hero; the other the procession of the Grail, followed by Amfortas, borne in as before on a litter.

The bier is erected in the middle of the stage in front of the altar and canopied throne. The song of the Knights follows; at its conclusion, Amfortas, raising himself on his couch, passionately invokes the spirit of his father, and, turning to the coffin, beseeches that the recovered vision of the Grail may bring to the Brotherhood the blessing of renewed life, to himself the deliverance of death. Importuned by the Knights to uncover the shrine, his resolution again fails him, and, throwing himself among them with bared breast, he bids them sheath their swords in his heart, and 'kill both the sinner and all his pain.' It is life, however, not death, that puts an end to pain—life more abundant, exuberant, victorious. The Knights fall back in dismay; and then Parsifal, accompanied by Gurnemanz and Kundry, advances, and, lowering the point of the holy Spear until it touches the wound of Amfortas, accomplishes the work of healing:

> One weapon only serves:
> The one that struck
> Can staunch thy wounded side.[1]

Wounds are in truth the remedy for wounds, tears for tears, mortification for mortal sin;

[1] Corder, p. 61.

but life is the bringer of the remedy; to put death to death is life's vocation. Amfortas knows within himself that he is healed of his plague, and a holy rapture of astonishment, issuing in grateful and adoring love, supersedes his despair. Parsifal at once pronounces his absolution, and, as he uplifts the Spear, all gaze upon it in ecstasy, recognizing in it the instrument of a Divine deliverance. The Spear-point is now seen to be touched with a rosy light, and to be pulsing, as the hand of Parsifal holds it aloft, with the very life of the Chalice. It suggests a deep theological truth; the Spear is really one with the Cross, it speaks of death; but, in the light of the all-illuminating Eucharist, the Cross is seen to be the tree of life, and the death, whose instrument it is, does but liberate the blood wherein the life resides. The fifth wound — the Spear-wound — inflicted after death, is in truth the prelude of the resurrection; it shows that death is impotent to arrest the victorious outflow and onrush of life—nay, more, that it is the necessary condition of its extended circulation. So the Divine Sacrament itself is not only the commemoration of a death, but the communication of a life; 'He became dead and is alive for evermore,' a life wherein all the members of His Mystical Body participate.

And now the end comes, a fitting consummation. Parsifal unveils the Grail, and kneels in silent prayer. The Knights and the assembled choirs, thrilled and awe-struck, follow his example, beholding this manifestation of the Divine Presence, so majestic in its simplicity, for

> This wondrous cup
> Is, like the golden vase in Aaron's ark,
> A fount of manna for a yearning world,
> As full as it can hold of God and heaven.[1]

[1] Hawker, *Cornish Ballads.*

The Cup, 'rose-red with beatings in it, as if alive,'[1] is elevated and waved (like the wave-offering of old) by the consecrated hands of Parsifal, and a white Dove descends from the dome and hovers over his head. Kundry, on her knees in adoration, advances to the altar, and falls dead at its foot; in company with the mother of sorrows and the father of heavenly dreams, she rests at last. Amfortas and Gurnemanz do homage on their knees to Parsifal. The Kingdom of love, joy, peace, righteousness, is established.

And so the great drama of human failure error, conflict, and temptation ends, by the Grace of God, not only in joy and victory, bu in worship and vision. The prayers, penances, and purifications of Good Friday have prepared the way for Easter peace and triumph the Divine Sacrament guarantees and enshrines an abiding presence; God's tabernacle

[1] Tennyson.

is with men; and the descending Dove, as
the curtain closes, speaks of the inauguration
of a Pentecostal ministry of power and consolation, whereby all things are renewed,
sanctified, and perfected. Death has become
the mother and minister of life, and life is
found to issue in a love-worship that satisfies,
in a beatific vision that endures. The Spear
is the sceptre of a King who reigns in
righteousness, and the Grail reveals and
communicates to men the Divine passion of
self-sacrificing love that eternally possesses
His Royal Heart. Softly and tenderly the
music, wafted from the summit of the dome,
dies away, accompanying the last words that
fall upon the ear—a prelude to the solemnity
of a great silence—' Salvation to the Saviour !'

It is the apocalyptic doxology, indicating
that the Saviour is Himself saved—a Divine
work only completed and concluded when all
whom His love has created and redeemed are

at length conformed to His likeness, and made partakers of His perfection.

'To him that overcometh will I give to eat of the tree of life, which is in the midst of the paradise of God.'

Deep calleth unto deep—God's deep
   To God-created depths in man ;
The hands that sow, the hands that reap,
   Complete what His began.

For His the seed, and His the fruit,
   And His the life at every stage ;
In God humanity strikes root,
   Evolved from age to age.

From age to age the vision grows ;
   Discerning eyes with wonder see
The desert blossom as the rose,
   God in humanity.

I hear a spirit-voice that calls
   To ears grown deaf, to hearts grown cold ;
'Tis music's spell, which still enthrals
   As sweetly as of old.

I find it wedded to the tale
  Oft told—a Gospel ever true—
The legend of the Holy Grail
  Interpreted anew.

Life conquers death in Parsifal,
  And Love, anointed priest and king,
Bids every heart keep festival,
  Bids all men pray and sing.

So evermore the vision grows ;
  Uplifted eyes with rapture see
The Chalice blushing as a rose
  Upon life's mystic Tree.

Deep answers deep—an antiphon
  More clearly heard from age to age ;
For God and man in Christ are one,
  And God man's heritage.

Bayreuth : August 15, 1888.

PRINTED BY
SPOTTISWOODE AND CO., NEW-STREET SQUARE
LONDON

www.ingramcontent.com/pod-product-compliance
Lightning Source LLC
Chambersburg PA
CBHW030024030726
47499CB00008B/3106